The Urbana Free Library

To renew: call 217-367-4057
or go to "*urbanafreelibrary.org*"
and select "Renew/Request Items"

Earning Excitement

By Paul Nourigat

Like most kids, Chelsea and Jack want stuff.

But they cannot afford everything they want.

How will they buy what they want,
when they don't have the money?

Illustrated by Natalie Nourigat

FarBeyond Publishing LLC

Earning Excitement

A big thank you goes out to my wife and kids,
clients, co-workers, friends, parents, grandparents,
teachers, and librarians who chimed in on
this important topic.

The illustrations in this book were inked by hand then
digitally colored by Natalie Nourigat,

Text and Illustrations Copyright © 2012 Paul Nourigat
Manufactured in USA

FarBeyond Publishing LLC

ISBN 978-1-936872-01-5

On a nice summer day, Chelsea and her brother Jack were having a great time at the playground. They had already played on the slides, monkey bars, and swings, when their neighbor Sebastian showed up with his new radio-controlled race car. He showed them how it worked, explaining, "It has a controller that you hold to steer the car left or right, and it also speeds up and slows down the car." Chelsea and Jack couldn't believe how much fun it was, and they started to really want a radio-controlled race car of their own.

2

That night, their parents helped Jack and Chelsea **research** radio-controlled race cars on the family computer. They found many different types of cars for many different **prices**, but really liked the Red Flyer Race Car. The best **value** was at a local store that charged thirty-eight dollars for the race car, rechargeable batteries and a carrying case.

The next day, Chelsea and Jack sat on the swings, talking. They felt a little stuck because they did not have thirty-eight dollars to buy the Red Flyer radio-controlled race car. They had spent their allowance on snacks and games, and their birthdays were still months away. They also didn't get as many gifts as Sebastian did. How would they buy the Red Flyer?

Jack wondered out loud, "Should we ask Mom and Dad to buy the radio-controlled race car?"

Chelsea and Jack's parents worked very hard at their jobs to buy their family's food, clothing, and housing, as well as gas for the car. Their mom was a **customer service** manager who talked to customers on the phone all day. Their dad worked for his **employer** as a sales representative who had to travel a lot to meet with clients.

Recently, Chelsea had heard their mom and dad agree to work hard to **save** their extra money so they could buy a new car.

Chelsea said, "Mom and Dad already do a lot for us. There must be a way that we can buy the Red Flyer on our own." Jack said, "If we had a job like Mom and Dad, we could buy things for ourselves." After a moment, they both jumped off the swings and cried out at the exact same time, "Let's get a job!" They ran home as fast as they could, excited to talk to their parents.

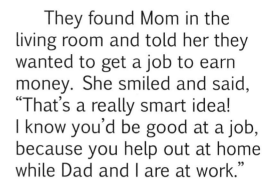

They found Mom in the living room and told her they wanted to get a job to earn money. She smiled and said, "That's a really smart idea! I know you'd be good at a job, because you help out at home while Dad and I are at work."

Chelsea and Jack cleaned up their own dishes every day, wiped off the counters, and vacuumed and swept the kitchen and living room.

Later that day, their dad returned home from a business trip. He also thought a job was a good idea. He said, "It feels good when people pay you to do a job. It also feels good to buy something with your own money."

After listening to him, Jack and Chelsea wondered, "What can we do to **earn** money?

Their friend Janet walked dogs and fed her neighbors' cats when the neighbors were on vacation. Their classmate James was a babysitter, taking care of younger kids while their parents were busy.

Their teenage cousin Craig **served** beverages at the cafe, and his friends worked at the grocery store. There were so many jobs in the world, but what could Chelsea and Jack do that people needed help with? How could they **earn** money for the Red Flyer?

Back at the playground, Chelsea and Jack spotted their friend Sebastian, who was playing with his race car again. "Hi," they said, and Sebastian waved.

He let them play with his car and, while he was watching them, he wiped his forehead, saying, "It's hot. I'm so thirsty."

Their letter carrier walked by the park and said hi to them. Jack and Chelsea noticed she was sweating from walking house to house, delivering mail in the warm weather.

She looked like she would really enjoy a cold drink.

Chelsea and Jack looked at each other, thinking. Then they both leapt off the ground at the same time and shouted, "I've got an idea!" Can you guess what their idea was?

"Let's sell drinks to people!" Chelsea and Jack said at the same exact time. They imagined all of the happy people cooling off with drinks Chelsea and Jack had sold to them.

Sebastian asked, "What kind of drinks will you sell?" and Jack asked, "How much money do you think people will pay us?" They realized that there were many questions they needed to answer to be sure they could do the job really well. It was time to **plan**!

Chelsea and Jack decided lemonade would be the best drink to sell. They agreed that it was easy to make, because it only required lemonade mix, water, ice, and a pitcher. Jack said, "People like healthy drinks, and lemonade will be better for them than soda-pop." Chelsea said, "You're right! This is going to be exciting!"

Jack and Chelsea's parents listened to their job idea and they discussed the things that would be needed. They agreed to let Chelsea and Jack use the family's plastic pitchers, card table, and chairs to set up their lemonade stand by the playground.

They also said they would buy the lemonade mix and the kids agreed to pay them back from their **profits**. What else would they need to do for a successful business?

Chelsea was very good with numbers, and figured out if they could **earn** enough money from selling lemonade. She added up the cost of the ingredients, and learned how many servings they could make from each packet of mix. Of course, they would also need cups, so she added the cost of buying those.

Jack was very good at drawing, so he began making a sign. It was big, so people could see it from far away, and it clearly described what they were selling. He also used bright colors, which he thought would catch people's attention.

18

Chelsea and Jack agreed that people would pay thirty-five cents for a cup of excellent lemonade. It would be cheaper than soda-pop, and also be at a **price** that kids and adults could **afford**.

But would charging thirty-five cents per cup be enough money to pay for their supplies and ingredients and still leave enough money to buy the Red Flyer?

Chelsea and Jack used math to figure out how many cups of lemonade they would have to sell so they could buy the Red Flyer radio-controlled race car. From the thirty-five cents per cup price, they subtracted the cost of supplies and ingredients that Chelsea had estimated earlier.

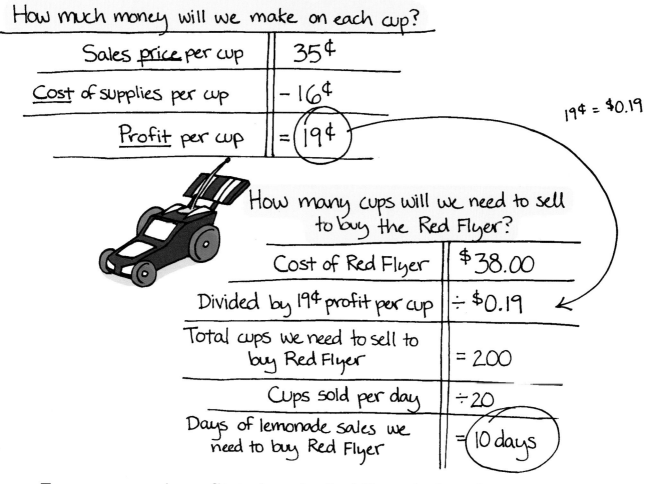

How much money will we make on each cup?

Sales price per cup	35¢
Cost of supplies per cup	− 16¢
Profit per cup	= 19¢

19¢ = $0.19

How many cups will we need to sell to buy the Red Flyer?

Cost of Red Flyer	$38.00
Divided by 19¢ profit per cup	÷ $0.19
Total cups we need to sell to buy Red Flyer	= 200
Cups sold per day	÷ 20
Days of lemonade sales we need to buy Red Flyer	= 10 days

To **earn** enough **profit** to buy the Red Flyer, Jack and Chelsea figured out that they would need to sell almost two hundred cups of lemonade. Do you think they could do that?

Chelsea and Jack are good at working as a team, and they realized their job was much easier if they each did different tasks.

Chelsea was good at some things, and Jack was good at other things. But they would both be good at playing with the Red Flyer!

The Big Day finally came! While Chelsea and Jack mixed up the first batch of lemonade, they couldn't stop smiling. They set up their stand by the playground, and waited patiently for their first **customer**.

Chelsea said, "Boy, it's hot."

Jack agreed and said, "People must be getting thirsty."

The letter carrier walked up and asked, "How much is your lemonade?" Jack smiled at her and said, "Thank you for asking. The **price** is thirty-five cents a cup."

The next thing they knew, they were pouring their first cup of lemonade for a **customer**! She paid them thirty-five cents, and said, "Thanks! I'll look for you tomorrow." Chelsea and Jack thanked her in return.

A couple of parents were leaving the playground with their kids, and they looked very tired. It must be hard work to keep an eye on kids and be sure that they're safe on the playground.

Before long, five more **customers** were drinking C&J's Excellent Lemonade!

By the time lunchtime was over, all three pitchers were empty and they had sold 20 cups! Thrilled, Jack and Chelsea took all of their supplies back home, then stacked and added up their money on the kitchen counter.

18 Quarters
$4.50

22 Dimes
$2.20

10 Nickels
$0.50

5 Pennies
$0.05

TOTAL=
$7.25

They had seven dollars from selling twenty cups of lemonade for thirty-five cents per cup, plus a tip. One **customer** gave them a tip of twenty-five cents.

How much money did we make on our first day?	
Sold 20 cups for 35¢ each	$7.00
Received a 25¢ tip for our huge smiles	+ .25
Total Sales	= $7.25
Pay back Mom and Dad for lemonade mix and cups	- $3.20
Total profit from first day's lemonade sales!!!!	$4.05

That night, Chelsea and Jack gave their parents $3.20 to pay them back for the lemonade mix. Their dad hugged them, smiling, and their mom said, "We're so proud of your success!" From their $4.05 **profit**, the kids would be able to buy more lemonade mix for the days ahead.

Jack and Chelsea noticed that many of the kids who drank their lemonade asked their parents for a snack. Lots of parents answered, "We'll have a snack when we get home."

After explaining this to their mom, she agreed to use the super secret family oatmeal cookie recipe and make cookies to help Chelsea and Jack's lemonade stand. Jack and Chelsea high-fived and went to work making cookies!

The next day, they sold twelve oatmeal cookies to **customers** who wanted a snack with their lemonade. They doubled their sales and made more money than they had expected. Awesome!

Some days, C&J's Excellent Lemonade sold faster than other days, and some days Mom's Famous Oatmeal Cookies were more popular. People loved the taste of the lemonade and the cookies, and they often said, "Your **prices** are very fair."

An elderly woman often sat alone on the park bench and watched them, but she never bought a drink of C&J's Excellent Lemonade or one of Mom's Famous Oatmeal Cookies. Jack said, "We should offer her a cup of lemonade and a cookie." Chelsea agreed with Jack's idea. The lady was very happy, and thanked them over and over.

Before long, Chelsea and Jack had **saved** thirty-eight dollars. They were excited when they took their money to the store and learned that the Red Flyer had gone on sale. The **price** had dropped from thirty-eight to thirty-four dollars. They would have extra money!

Chelsea said, "Let's **save** the extra money for our school carnival." Jack agreed. "Then we'll be able to buy more carnival game tickets!"

It was really fun to be able to race cars with Sebastian and build roads and obstacle courses for the race cars to drive around. Chelsea and Jack learned a job can be fun and rewarding. They were proud that they had earned the money to buy their own car.

They were already thinking about school starting and the big school carnival. They were so glad they had already begun **saving** for that new adventure! Do you think they will succeed in their goal to **save** enough money for the carnival?

Financial Glossary

Not sure what that word meant? Below are some important words and concepts used in this book and their definitions:

Afford ... Having enough money to pay for something.

Customer ... Someone who pays you money for a product or service.

Earn ... Doing something for which you expect to be paid.

Employer ... A company who pays an employee to work.

Paycheck ... How most people get paid after doing their jobs.

Plan ... Helps people decide if an idea will work.

Price ... The amount of money it costs to buy something.

Profit ... The amount of money left over after paying for the costs of your business (such as the ingredients for lemonade)

Saving ... Money that's set aside and not spent right away.

Serve ... When you help someone with something.

Research ... To study something and learn more about it.

Value ... Buying a product or service for a fair price.

Tips for Kids
The Recipe For Doing A Good Job

Learn what your customer wants
> Consider what people want, so you can help them.

Do what you say you will do
> Do what you agreed to do. When your customers need help again, they'll think of you.

Be friendly while you are working
> People like to do business with friendly people. Always try to be polite and kind. People will appreciate your smile.

Thank your customer for the opportunity
> When someone pays you for something, they have helped you. Be sure to thank your customers.

Ask your parents
> It's important to talk with your parents about jobs, because they have already worked in many kinds of jobs. They can help you decide what jobs you will do, whom you will work with, and how much you should be paid.

Learn more about jobs for kids at www.MarvelsOfMoney.org

Tips for Parents
How to encourage great earning habits

Talk about your job

> Regardless of what your job is, you can teach your children important lessons using your day-to-day activities at work. If there is an opportunity to take your children to work occasionally, do so. Exposing them to your workplace will give them confidence in the years ahead, even if they choose a different path.

Help your child evolve into jobs

> As children grow up, more and more jobs will become available to them. Start building work ethic early with chores around the house and running errands, while taking a bit of extra time to explain things as you go. Small experiences add up and can make a difference.

Encourage ambition

> By applauding a child for jobs or chores done well, you are reinforcing their success habits. When they stretch and fail, emphasize the positive, balanced with light constructive suggestions to improve.

Work together

> While it is ok to tell a kid how to work, it is best to show them as they often learn more from watching and experiencing than they learn from listening.

Find great resources and tools at www.MarvelsOfMoney.org

About the author

Paul Nourigat has advised families, businesses, and community leaders across the country for over 28 years.

In addition to his time spent with thousands of highly successful people, he has invested extensive time with families who are struggling with money. As a result, Paul developed a clear understanding of "what works" and "what doesn't" in business and personal finance.

Having heard over and over "I wish I had learned more about money when I was young", he set out on a mission to teach young people about money using a very unique approach. Blending extensive graphics and fictional stories which young people connect with, Paul is breaking new ground by using the graphic novel format to teach financial literacy.

About the illustrator

Natalie Nourigat is a recent college graduate enjoying financial independence and her career as a freelance artist. At 16, she created her first website, where she began publishing and selling her artwork.

She enjoys earning a living doing what she loves, in the vibrant community of artists in Portland, Oregon.

Natalie's many other works can be found at natalienourigat.com

Books from the author

"Why is there Money?" (For younger readers, ages 5-8 years)
This poetic journey through history shows the path from bartering to currencies, to credit, to the modern financial tools used by adults. Kids will enjoy the beautiful original images as they visualize the fascinating evolution of world commerce.

"Marvels of Money ... for kids" (For young readers 7-12 years)
Richly illustrated, engaging and practical stories for young readers about the fundamentals of money. Five stories follow Chelsea and Jack through life experiences which kids will recognize, while showing how they deal with financial struggles, decisions and actions. 200 pages of engaging original illustrations, fictional stories, glossaries for new vocabulary and even a "Tips for Parents" section!

"Earning Excitement", "Spending Success", "Debt Dangers", "Giving Greatness", and "Terrific Tools for Money" are available as separate books or combined in a 5 story book.

"If Money Could Shout: the brutal truths for teens" (For readers 13-19 years)
A breakthrough graphic novel for teens and young adults about money and the choices which will affect their lives in a big way. Eight fictional stories illustrated by eight talented artists from diverse parts of the United States. Over 400 vivid illustrations compliment the eight captivating stories about the lives of teens and how they deal with financial decisions. Visually stunning, deep in messaging, highly engaging for young people who would love an alternative to a "text book" on the topic of personal finance and life success.